FELIX

Giovanna Zoboli

Illustrated by
Simona Mulazzani

Translated by
Laura Watkinson

Eerdmans Books for Young Readers

Grand Rapids, Michigan

There was once a fine city cat whose name was Felix.

Felix had lots of friends—a balcony, two books, some cushions, a window (and, in that window, the night and the moon), a brush, his owner's legs, and (a long time ago, when he was small) a little ball as well.

One summer it was very hot. All the ceiling fans were on, turning and turning, around and around. It seemed as if the city might fly away at any moment.

Where to? wondered Felix.

Felix looked at a map of the world and saw India with its golden temples, China with its wide rivers, Russia with its freezing winters, America with its deep canyons, Brazil with its deafening rain forests, Ethiopia with its violet volcanoes . . .

I have lots of family out there, he remembered. His mother had told him so on the very first day of his life, the day when a cat receives the gifts of charm and grace.

And since he had only two of his nine lives left, Felix decided it was time to go visit his family. So he left the way cats always leave when they want to see the world—silently, through a little door in the darkness.

When Felix arrived in India, it was dawn.

Mrs. Tiger was cooking shrimp and scrambled eggs, while
Mr. Tiger was hanging the washing, and the three little tiger cubs
were squabbling.

"Be good, children," Mr. Tiger said. "Your Uncle Felix has come to
visit. Say hello to him and go wash your paws."

Then they all sat down to eat their toast, eggs, and shrimp, and drink
their mango juice.

"Where do you live, Uncle Felix?" asked the first tiger cub.

"Are you married, Uncle Felix?" asked the second tiger cub.

"Why are you so small, Uncle Felix?" asked the third tiger cub.

"Stop asking questions, you cheeky little cubs," said Mrs. Tiger.

"And finish your breakfast."

When breakfast was over, Felix politely said goodbye. "I really think I should be going now. It's getting late. Thank you for your hospitality, my dear cousins. I've been wanting to meet you for such a long time. I've heard so much about your sharp teeth and your fearsome eyes, but you're even more magnificent than I ever imagined."

"Did you hear that, children?" said Mr. Tiger. "Say thank you to Uncle Felix, who's come all the way from the other side of the world. So much kindness in such a tiny ball of fur!"

"Goodbye, Uncle Felix! Thank you, Uncle Felix! Safe travels, Uncle Felix!" the three little tiger cubs called.

Mrs. Tiger gave Felix a lotus flower for the journey.

Because tigers can be kind and gentle when they want to be.

China's rivers are huge! So big that Felix couldn't quite believe his eyes. Its mountains are enormous too, rising up high and vanishing into the clouds. Up there lived some of his most mysterious cousins—the snow leopards. Felix went to visit their icy home.

"Welcome, Felix. Make yourself at home. Would you like a cup of tea and some herring, my dear cousin? I had a fresh delivery from the Bering Strait this morning."

Felix didn't need to be asked twice. As he nibbled at the herrings on the tip of his fork, he watched his hosts. "You're so refined and elegant. You look like you're ready to host royalty!" he said.

Mrs. Snow Leopard laughed. "Host royalty? You are too kind!" she said. "Actually, all we're ready for is our afternoon nap. If you want gorgeous fur, you need a lot of beauty sleep."

Before leaving the snow leopards, Felix thanked them both. "I knew you were beautiful, but seeing you for real is amazing."

Mr. and Mrs. Snow Leopard each gave him a hug, both feeling delighted because they were very vain. "This is for you," they said. "It's a peony from our valley." Felix thought about the wonderful story he'd have to tell his friends the cushions, who had a soft spot for the aristocracy.

By that afternoon, Felix was already in the Russian steppes. *Look at all that lovely snow!* he thought, his heart as light as a snowflake. He stepped off the train at afternoon snack time, feeling a little hungry.

If I'm not mistaken, he said to himself, walking into the forest, *this is the right place.*

Sure enough, before long he saw a cozy yurt. *Knock-knock.*

"My dear cousin!" exclaimed Mr. Lynx. "Please come in! I've been expecting you. I just finished making blinis, in fact. They're delicious with caviar. Do have a taste."

Later he showed Felix his family album. "There's Aunt Olga! And Aunt Tatiana! They taught me everything I know."

When the snack was finished, Felix gave his cousin a hug. "I'd heard so much about your beautiful ears and fur, but seeing them for myself is something else!"

"You're so delightfully charming," said Mr. Lynx. "Allow me to give you this sprig of birch. And say hello to the city lights for me. Sometimes I dream about them, you know. I've heard how lovely they are."

When Felix reached the deserts of the United States, it was sunset. He had never seen a red quite so red before. The clouds were on fire! And the horizon was more horizontal than anywhere he had ever been. His cousin Mr. Puma welcomed him to his home.

"Please, Felix, sit wherever you like. As you can see, there's plenty of space here. It'll be dinnertime soon, and I'll serve you up a fabulous steak."

Feeling very happy indeed, Felix settled down to admire the view.

As he was enjoying his steak, Felix sneaked a peek at his blond and breezy cousin. *He's not that different from me,* he thought to himself. *He moves between cactus and canyon the same way I move between cushion and cat basket.*

Before long, it was time to say goodbye. Mr. Puma gave Felix a twinkly smile. "Do you know something, Cousin Felix?" he said. "The two of us are really quite similar. There's not that much difference between your cozy chair and my warm rocks."

From there Felix traveled on to the immense rain forests of Brazil. Darkness had fallen by that time, but the panther was even darker than the dark, dark night.

"Shh! Would you please be quiet, cousin? We're not up on some city roof here. Be careful where you put your paws, too. If you want to prowl the moonless night, you have to be more nimble than a moth, more invisible than a chameleon, more stealthy than a snake."

Felix felt embarrassed. He'd always thought he was a master of balance, dexterity, and grace, but this lady dressed in black was the essence of shadow. He was very sorry indeed.

"Oh, you don't need to apologize," she said. "I'm far too demanding. Why don't you climb up onto this branch? I've prepared some kebabs for a midnight snack that I'm sure you'll enjoy."

Time passed swiftly and quietly beneath all those millions of stars.

"I have to go now," Felix finally whispered. "I knew that you were mysterious, my cousin, but now I know that your home is in the very heart of the night." And the panther, feeling happy and drowsy, said, "Oh, hush now, Cousin Felix. Take this—it's a passion flower. It'll remind you of our meal together."

When Felix arrived in the African savannah, the sun was already shining high in the sky, and everything was rippling in the heat. The lion family was resting beneath an acacia tree. Felix crept closer. His night without sleep had tired him out, not to mention all those miles traveling around the world. He yawned.

"May I?" he timidly asked an old lioness.

"Please do, Cousin Felix," she replied. "Just choose a nice shady spot and close your eyes."

Within a minute, Felix was asleep.

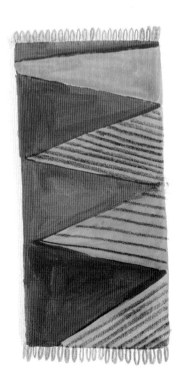

How wonderful to sleep like that, all together: dreams mix and mingle, and no one knows which dream is whose. When you wake up, you realize that you've become a little more like your brothers and sisters, your aunts and uncles, your grandmothers and grandfathers, and even more like your ancestors.

Maybe, thought Felix in his sleep, *the savannah has one big dream every night and everyone who lives there dreams that same dream all together.*

But now it was time to return home.

Felix didn't want to wake anyone. He left on the tips of his toes, but not without saying goodbye, since he was a very polite cat. "Thank you, my wonderful cousins. I knew your roaring was regal, but your deep, deep yawns are filled with the sweetness of sleep. I'll take this acacia branch as a reminder of you."

Back on his balcony, Felix looked out at the city.

What a wonderful view!

He was so happy to be home.

He told the cushions about the snow leopards.

He told his balcony about the sleeping lions, and his owner's legs about the joy of thick, soft fur.

And so, dear reader, when in the future you can't find your cat, and you've looked twenty times in your drawers, in your closets, under the bed, among your socks, in the pots and pans, in the broom closet, in the basement, behind the bookcase and the washing machine, behind the dishwasher and the oven, below the stairs, on the roof, in the gutter, in the bushes, in your neighbor's garden, down the street, under the cars parked outside . . .

When, after doing all of that, you still haven't found your cat, and you're beginning to think the worst, and you're forced, for the thirtieth time, to search

in your drawers,

in your closets,

under the bed,

among your socks,

in the pots and pans,

in the broom closet,

in the basement,

behind the bookcase and the washing machine,

behind the dishwasher and the oven,

below the stairs,

on the roof,

in the gutter,

in the bushes,

in your neighbor's garden,

down the street,

under the cars parked outside . . .

When that happens, remember that when cats want to leave, they do so silently, the way cats always leave when they want to see the world—through a little door in the darkness. And while you're at home worrying, your cat just might be off eating midnight snacks in Brazil, prawns and scrambled eggs in India, blinis and caviar in Russia, or tea and herring from the Bering Strait in China.

Or maybe your cat is somewhere in Africa, sunk in a dreamy sleep
under an acacia tree.

Remember that. And be patient.